## The English Lesson

Sara Alexi is the author of the Greek Village Series.
She divides her time between England and a small
village in Greece.

http://facebook.com/authorsaraalexi

Sara Alexi

# THE ENGLISH LESSON

## A Novella

oneiro

Published by Oneiro Press 2015

ISBN-13: 978-1511988797

ISBN-10: 1511988797

Also by Sara Alexi

# Juliet

The sun reflects off the water, almost blinding Juliet as she eases her old car into a spot by the harbour wall. Over the cracking plastic dashboard and through the dust-smeared windscreen, the sea's surface shimmers. The late summer heat is still stifling as August temperatures linger on.

A fishing boat amongst the few remaining tourist yachts bobs and wallows lazily. The fisherman on board moves without haste, his net between his toes, his hands maintaining tension as he weaves, making good last night's damage. He looks up, nods his recognition to Juliet, and glances briefly at Michelle.

Michelle links Juliet's arm as they dodge tanned men on mopeds to cross the road to the cafés. Juliet leads away from the touristy coffee houses and tavernas in by the harbour.

'I thought we were going for coffee?' Michelle releases Juliet's arm to put her hand up to shade her eyes from the sun, scanning the lines of comfy chairs. Waiters beckon, music seeps towards them, cats wind around table legs with promises of love in return for food. The place is pleasantly empty of tourists this early in the day, this late in the year.

Juliet ignores the temptation and leads the way down a narrow side road to the lane that runs behind the relatively noisy promenade. Without the chrome and glass facades, it is easier to appreciate the beauty of these big, Venetian-influenced buildings. They are solid and square, made from cut, yellowish stone. Some are two storeys high, some three. Ornate embellishments decorate the lintels, and marble cantilevered balconies hang over the road. On the ground floor, are several archways leading into each building. Intricately carved double doors give access to the ground level and the stairs to the apartments above. High up against the blue sky, fancy brickwork under the eaves suggests the original grandeur of these homes. The majority have grey or the palest of blue shutters over closed windows on the upper floors. The architecture is of a past era, built by ship owners and businessmen after Greece was liberated from Turkish rule and before the economic crash.

Michelle hurries to catch Juliet.

'This lady, Toula, suggested a new café round the back here.' Juliet waits for Michelle.

'I thought she was from our village?' Michelle has almost caught up with her.

'She is—was—but her husband did well and they moved into town. Been here most of her married life, I believe.' Juliet moves with long, languid strides as if the heat has sucked the haste from her. Her pale, loose clothes flow as she moves.

The lane is too narrow for cars, giving the appearance that it has been pedestrianised, although mopeds still weave past. The noises from the harbour are muffled now they have turned the corner, leaving an air of peace and tranquility.

A man wearing black trousers, a white shirt, and a narrow white apron comes hurrying past them. He has a key in his hand and, with a well-practiced movement, he opens one of the grand, ground level doors to reveal a wide, sweeping staircase, the shine of wood glimmering in the darkness. The waiter strides into the gloom and returns presently, wobbling with the weight of a crate of beer in one hand and a stack of pressed and clean tablecloths in the other. He takes the time to smile at them both in his hurry, but his presence shatters the illusion of the mansion's continued opulence. The upper stories are now broken up into storage units for the cafés and tavernas below. Juliet knows that the Port Police offices take up the whole of one upper floor of

5

one of the buildings. A notorious lawyer has another. She has heard that is difficult to live in these upper floors now because of the noise generated by the cafés below in the small hours of the morning. Occasionally she has spotted little old ladies, dressed in black, slipping, like mice, out of the majestic doorways. Sometimes they lean over one of the balcony railings to haul shopping up in wicker baskets. But that is a rare sight these days.

Those that remain must struggle with the cost of maintenance as the ornate stonework crumbles in the sea air, the roofs almost impossible to get to in order to repair. To her knowledge, there is only one mansion where the whole of the two upper floors retain their residential status and that is owned by Toula, the lady she is due to meet.

'She lives here, I believe.' Juliet points at a pair of neatly trimmed box trees that stand sentinel either side of elaborately carved and freshly painted wooden double doors. A cat is curled up on the doorstep.

'Oh, what a lovely place to live.' Michelle looks up at Toula's balconies with their fancy iron railings. All the houses on the street, both the grand ones on the right and the more modest dwellings on the left, have balconies. Those on

6

the left, away from the noise of the cafés—smaller, newer, cheaper—are lived in and consequently, their balconies explode with well-tended bougainvillea. The trailing plants have been hooked across the road to create tunnels of colour interspersed between patches of sunlight. Toula's is the only balcony on the right that has done the same. Her bougainvillea is pale orange. Halfway across the void, it intertwines with a pink plant and the colours merge in a shocking contrast.

'Is that the café?' Michelle points ahead to two tables and four chairs tucked under a vine that trails to the floor.

'I guess so.' There is no sign to indicate it is a café.

'She's an old lady, you said?'

'It's hard to tell on the phone, but by the way she was talking, reminiscing about the village, my guess is that she won't be young.'

'It seems odd that she wants to bother with English lessons if she is really old.'

'Once fifty was a very old age to live to. Now, people like us are uprooting and moving abroad at that age.' Juliet pulls out a chair and sits. Michelle does the same, tucking a vine tendril back on itself so it is out of her way.

'So tell me, how was summer?' Once seated, Juliet starts the conversation with energy.

'Good. No, great! I wondered a couple of times if I had done the right thing. You know, having a house in the village over here and the bed and breakfast over on Orino island, but now I am back for the winter, I feel more sure. I definitely need a break from the island now the season is over. Even if my home wasn't here, I would definitely go off somewhere, but having the village to return to is so... What's the right word? Grounding? Stabilising? Relaxing?' She shrugs.

'Well, your home is here and what's more, it was very successful as a holiday let over the summer. I even filled that gap of three days you had back in June,' Juliet says as she scans the menu. 'Now you have done a season, do you feel you made the right choice to sell up in the UK?' She looks up, waiting for the reply.

Putting down the menu, Michelle looks up at the blue sky between the orange tiled roofs.

'Without hesitation, yes! The real question is why I didn't do it earlier like you. Fear of the unknown, I suppose. You know what I do miss about my old life, though?'

'No, what?' There is a chuckle in her throat as she says this, as if she is ready for the punchline.

'Nothing,' Michelle scoffs.

Whenever they are together, it never takes long before they drift into behaving without any sense, teenagers again. The years pass, their experiences grow, but it all drops away once they are together.

They laugh in unison at their mutual childish sense of humour, and the waiter who has come out to take their order smiles to join in and waits for their merriment to subside before he asks what they want. After he returns inside, Juliet continues.

'I do want to hear more details about your summer. But mostly...' Juliet lowers her voice and leans towards Michelle. 'Have you heard from Dino?'

'Well, we agreed we wouldn't write.' The words are stiff.

'You agreed that you wouldn't write, but I wasn't so sure that he was going to stick with your rules.'

Michelle takes a deep breath and lets it out noisily through her nose as she starts to shake her head.

'I feel so bad. There's not a day that has passed since he left that I have not thought about him. But, I mean, he's just a boy. He needs a life, not an old hag like me. But I can't seem to let him go. I know it would only take one move from him and all my resolution would be gone.'

'Hey, less of the "old," please. Remember we are the same age.' Juliet tries to lighten the mood, but Michelle does not even smile.

'It was just a summer romance, a fling, a little fantasy.' Michelle continues to shake her head as she speaks.

'I really don't think it was, for him.'

Michelle looks down into her lap and a shadow crosses her face.

'Hey, what is it?' Juliet leans over and puts a hand on her friend's arm.

Michelle looks up and flashes a smile. 'I'm alright, really. Sorry. I'm being silly. But you know, since they stationed him in Preveza…'

'Oh, I thought he was at the barracks in Thessaloniki?'

'He was, but you know, they move them around every month or so, and his friend Adonis told me that he is now in Preveza. But even that was a couple of months ago, and I don't really know. I mean, a part of me wants him to forget about me, but a part of me hurts, too. Is that very selfish?'

Juliet shakes her head. 'No, no, Mich. That's not selfish. I think that has another word...'

Michelle's eyes flash as she looks at Juliet, a warning, a spark of hope. She is not sure.

'Here you go.' The waiter's voice is bright as he returns with two cold coffees. Juliet and Michelle sit back and, with a glance at each other, their conversation drops for the moment.

The waiter has also brought glasses of iced water for them both and a plate of small biscuits. He gently fusses about, trying to find room on the small table. He has grey flecks in his hair and a softness of manner, and a smile that lights up his face as he works. A movement takes Juliet's gaze past him, along the street to a woman with a bad stoop who is closing the door to the end building, and a little shiver runs down her spine.

'What's up?' Michelle asks, following her gaze. The waiter leaves.

'I guess that's her. Toula,' Juliet replies and shivers again.

'Yes, but why did you shiver?'

'I'm not sure. Just when I saw her, I had the strangest of feelings, like someone had walked over my grave. Actually, not so much my grave as someone else's.'

'Wierdo,' Michelle says, but Juliet does not smile.

They sip their coffees and watch as the old woman makes her way towards them. She stops to pet the cat that was curled on her doorstep, fussing over it. She bends down and picks up a paper bag that someone has scrunched and dropped. Then she goes in another door.

'I think she has stood you up,' Michelle says.

'Isn't that the office of the electrician?' Juliet asks.

The old woman comes out again, the paper bag no longer in her hand, and her progress continues. Michelle and Juliet continue to watch and sip their coffees. The woman's progress is very slow. She stops again and pinches off a flower from a white bougainvillea before continuing on her way.

'She looks harmless enough to me,' says Michelle, putting one of the small biscuits into her mouth whole. Each of the old woman's steps has a little shake at the end and her head judders from side to side, her eyes forced on the ground by the curve of her back. It is only when she is some feet away that she makes an attempt to straighten up. She catches Juliet's eye and the smile this ignites is so bright and warm, both Michelle and Juliet exhale at the same time.

Michelle leans back in her chair, relaxed, and Juliet leans forward to greet the newcomer.

# Toula

'Well girls, hello!' Toula says in English. 'Juliet, I presume?' Juliet is exactly as she imagined her to be from the phone calls. She seems very English somehow, with her long golden blond hair. Toula notices there are touches of grey at her temples. Her dress is loose linen in a very pale sand colour, almost white. Her sandals look like they have seen a few years of wear and her toenails are neat but unpolished.

The woman she is with holds her shoulders a little higher, her back a little straighter, less relaxed. But again, somehow, obviously English. The slightest of breezes teases at the branches of a vine that casts a dappled shade across the two of them.

'And this lovely lady is?' Toula turns after shaking Juliet's hand to look at her friend.

'Kyria Toula, this is Michelle,' Juliet introduces them.

'Michelle *hero poly*.' Toula doesn't notice that she has slipped back into her mother tongue.

'*Episis*,' Michelle responds.

'English?' Juliet says gently.

'Yes, you are right, it is so easy to, ah, what is the word, to move easily, to...'

'Slip?'

14

'Yes, that is the word. It is so easy to slip into Greek. But as it comes back to me, I will remember more.' Yes, if Juliet is strict with her, this could work out very well.

'Right.' Michelle stands. 'Lovely to meet you, Kyria Toula, but I promised myself that I would look around the shops today. It is a while since I was here and I want to re-familiarise myself with everything.' Michelle takes a last suck on her straw to get to the bottom of the iced coffee before replacing the glass on the table.

'Oh, please do not feel that is necessary.' It would be a shame if Juliet's friend were to leave on her account. If she stays, it might even be better, for the first lesson, to listen to the two of them talk.

Toula's head wobbles from side to side. It does that when she gets excited. It is a small movement, a tremor, but she has no control over it. All she can do is hope neither Juliet nor Michelle have noticed.

'Thank you, but there are one or two things I need to do.' Michelle smiles at them both, her eyes narrowed against the sun, and wanders away.

Toula shuffles into the vacated seat as Juliet looks around for the waiter.

When he comes, Toula orders a Greek coffee.

'So, let's see how much English you know and then I can work out how we should best proceed,' Juliet says with a smile.

'Just to chat will be fine.'

'Well, I would find it useful to know the extent of your English. Let's start with you telling me why you want to learn English and where you have learnt what you know so far and what you will use it for in the future. That should cover all tenses.'

'Oh, I see. Okay.' She is going to enjoy this. 'I learnt English in school.'

'In the village?'

'Yes. Then I married and my English was for my husband's work. He builted one house...' She gesticulates, hoping to make up for her bad English. She steeples her fingers to put on an imaginary roof to the house she has just drawn out. 'I sell it to Americans and with the money, he builded two more. I sell to very nice Australian and to very nice American. I am liking to think it is my English that makes good prices.' She opens her hands, palms upwards, and shrugs her shoulders. She will never know for sure. 'But if it was or no, the prices make him to build more. But this was a long time ago...' She points her fingers over her shoulders and shakes her head to show how long ago this all was.

As she does so, the years fall away as she recalls her youth, the early days of her marriage. She remembers a touch of the joy and the enthusiasm that she and Apostolis shared when working together back then. That was before he met George, the architect from Athens. The feeling of joy evaporates. How quickly she was squeezed out of her own world then, from business partner to cook and cleaner in six months. Her newlywed life being replaced by a sadness that she never, not for a second, expected to stay with her all these years.

'Why do you want to improve your English now, and what will you do with this language in the future?' Juliet asks. The waiter brings a small cup that has a million shiny bubbles on the surface.

'Oh bravo,' Toula says. 'For every bubble, you are having a coin.' She quotes the Greek prophesy in English and then winks at the waiter, who nods and leaves. The cat from the lane has followed her and sits patiently between the chairs. She reaches down and plays with its ears.

'Oh yes.' Toula returns her focus to the lesson. 'I want make better my English because before four years, my daughter she married the English man. They are living in London. One day maybe she comes here with my grandchildren. I want to speak with them.'

'You want to be able to speak to them,' Juliet corrects softly.

'Yes, I do!' Toula raises her eyebrows. Why would she question this point? But then she lowers them and nods. Juliet is making a point about her grammar! 'Ah yes, I want to be able to,' she repeats. It's like being back at school.

'Have you been to London?' Juliet asks.

'No. They marry here. I see the first grandchild, Katerina, when she come here and she was one years old. She is perfect.' It takes a moment or two to leave thoughts of Katerina behind. 'But I do not see little Apostolis. Katerina is three this month.' A familiar tension pulls at her chest. 'I very much want to go the London and see them. But my husband, he does not want. He does not speak English and he would not like to...' Toula stops speaking, her sentence unfinished. What wouldn't he like? To be out of Greece. To be out of control? To not be in charge? To be one of thousands of foreigners in England?

'Are you lost for a word?' Juliet asks.

'No.' Toula sighs and looks at her watch.

'We have lots of time.' Juliet says, with which Toula lets her shoulders drop and gives up trying to think of the word she needs to explain Apostolis.

Juliet is smiling.

Generally, her new teacher seems very unpretentious and seems to have a warm heart. But, and she is very aware of this, her biggest attraction to Juliet is that she is not Greek. This is not her attraction as a teacher, but as someone to spend time with. She is not of her circle, or to be more accurate, Apostolis' circle of friends. She could tell Juliet anything and it would not be passed around the tight-knit group she and Apostolis make company with by the end of the day.

'I used to live in the village. The village you live now.'

Juliet nods. It encourages her to keep trying with her English although she is tiring already. It takes so much effort to remember the English words.

'I grew up the village. Also Apostolis. My husband.' She might have told Juliet this over the phone, but she cannot remember.

Juliet gives her another nod and moves her chair a little into the shade.

'We are at school together. We work hard, make money. We moved here, Saros town. Now we live in a big house, alone. Next house is no one.' She wonders if she can explain that all she can see in her future is more and more isolation. But as she doesn't know the English world for isolation, it remains unsaid.

'Okay. So we are going to do a little work on the past tense,' Juliet says with a brief glance to the vine above her head, which is not doing much of a job of blocking the sun from her eyes. She moves her chair again, then crosses her ankles and leans over to write in her notebook on her knee.

Toula watches the pen move in squiggles across the page. The weight of her sadness, her constant companion, lifted momentarily when she met Juliet, but now it has returned. It is not Juliet's fault. Of course not. How could it be? It is just how things are, how they have been for years. Years and years. Years and years and years …

# Juliet

'How did it go?' Michelle holds several stiff bags with rope handles in each hand.

'Did you leave anything in the shops?' Juliet quips.

'Listen, a whole summer on Orino island running the hotel made no time for shopping. So what was Toula like as a student? Are you glad you took her on?'

'Oh, she's a lovely lady, but with a real deep strain of melancholy about her. I got the impression that she does not feel that she has lived the life she wanted somehow.'

'Oh dear. So why is she learning English at this time in her life?'

'English grandchildren. Do you want to eat here, somewhere else, or go home?'

'Somewhere else, I think. Has she been to England then?'

'No, her husband is not keen.'

'She should dump him and move countries like we did.' Michelle closes her eyes as she laughs. It is a laugh of relief. They have both done it. They have both moved on from bad marriages and had the courage to follow their dreams. They can afford to laugh.

'I am beginning to think living in Greece is making you a bit wild. Talking of which, you still haven't told me if you have decided to contact Dino or not?'

'I'll go in and pay.' Michelle sidles past Juliet, leaving her bags behind on the table.

# Toula

The door needs a little shove to open it fully. It was the same last year. As soon as summer has gone, the wood absorbs the sea air and expands. The bottom edge scrapes slightly on the worn tiles. Why Apostolis won't let her get a carpenter to shave a little off the bottom, goodness only knows.

She takes a final look down the street back at the café. It is strange to have someone to talk to who knows nothing about her and who has no reverence for Apostolis.

The cat is at her ankles again, nuzzling her for attention. It is not as if it would do any harm to let it in. She can see Apostolis' point about the cat hair, but it is such a friendly thing.

The temperature drops as she steps inside. The hall on the north side is the first part of the house to become cold. If it has a chill there, then she knows August has truly passed. These houses get so hot in the summer, but like ice in the winter.

Looking up the wide wooden staircase, its carved handrail polished with time and use, she wonders if she can manage them today. Usually, she makes herself climb them for the exercise but just now, everything seems different somehow, as if she has lost all will to make any extra effort. Her meeting with Juliet has highlighted for her the feelings she has spent so long trying to ignore.

Turning away from the stairs, and with a degree of trepidation, she slides the metal concertina gate open and pulls on the shiny brass handles to open the wooden doors into the lift. The floor is tilted at an angle. This is not a good thing, but then, if the first of the rains were to come now, at least the water wouldn't be able to pool on the lift floor as it did at this time last year. The cat would sneak in and drink from the puddle and Toula would chase it out, worried it might get shut in. In the end, a bowl of milk on the street solved the problem.

She really must ask the electrician again to try and prioritise this job. Surely it is not safe like this? If only Apostolis would have a word with him, she feels sure he would do it today, as a priority!

Stepping inside, she closes the gate and hesitates before pressing the button with the scrolled lettering *Pano* cast in brass relief around it. The word *Kato* circles a second button. The brass shines in the half gloom. With just a little pressure from her forefinger, the cogs begin to turn; the chains rattle. Her grip on the handrail tightens as the floor straightens and the counterweight begins to move. The wooden cage jerks and begins to lift.

Apostolis had the lift installed for his mama when they first bought the place. Toula used to run up the steps then. Now her feet stand where her mother-in-law's once stood and her pace is as slow as the old woman's before her. She never thought she would see the day when she, too, would be that old.

A rattle of chains and a judder of the floor, and the ornamental crate comes to a standstill, not quite level with the polished wood of the first floor. It has stopped too soon again. Last week, it stopped so if she hitched up her skirts and took a big step she was out, but today, the height is more than she can manage. The room looks odd from this low angle.

The floor boards, old and dark, waver over the beams, rising and falling like the sea. Time has warped the straightness out of them. The dark wood panelling of the walls and dark wood furniture give the room a heavy feel. The oil paintings around the wall do nothing to lift the sombre appearance. The slices of sun through the louvred shutters only accentuate the stillness. There are very few dust mites dancing in the air. Apostolis likes her to dust every day with a damp cloth. The only colour in the room is from the armchairs that she sewed covers for, oh, over ten years ago now. Apostolis hated the bright fabric when she first did it, but age has dulled them and the flowers are pastel shades now. They are only slightly less dull than the rest of the decor.

The heat gets trapped in this room with its windows that face south, over the sea. It is like a greenhouse until the cold Northern wind creeps in from the back, chasing the heat out for another winter.

'Apostolis, are you there?' Her voice sounds muffled by the lift shaft but she knows the acoustics will carry the sound. She listens, but all she can hear is the ticking of his clocks, time passing. She looks at her watch. It is very nearly mid-day. If he does not hear her before the first clock begins to strike, she could be here for some time. Her suggestion that he gets them to strike all at the same time seems incomprehensible to him.

'Apostolis.' She raises her voice to a shout but she has such little volume these days and not much power to her lungs. She presses the up button hard, and a couple of more times as well, to be sure. The counterweight drops, she grips the handrail, and the floors become more level.

Smoothing her skirts, she sits on the first floor as if it is a chair and then attempts to spin around, but it is hard to get her legs up. She is not as supple as she was.

'What on earth are you doing?' His indignant tone shows no compassion. She stops trying to help herself.

'I went into the electrician's today. They say they can come out next week, but if we are going to use it, we should get it working properly and ensure that it is safe sooner.' Toula holds a hand up, inviting Apostolis to help her up.

'I never seem to have a problem.' He takes his fob watch from his waistcoat pocket and presses the latch to open the silver cover. He looks around the room expectantly as the first clock begins to chime. Toula closes her eyes and waits. The mantel clock is first, but is soon interrupted by the English long-case clock. An ornate Swiss affair joins the cacophony and then the French brass carriage clock adds its more refined tones. One from his study strikes and the skeleton clock in the kitchen joins in. The modern 'art piece', as Apostolis refers to the huge abstract thing on the wall, adds a bass tone.

Away in the distance, from the floor above, in their grand bedroom and the unused guest rooms, other clocks join in, adding layers to what is already a deafening sound.

Toula waves her hand at him but he is lost in his orchestral composition.

'Tolis!' she shouts, edging her words with the coarse accent of the village. He jumps, remembers she is there, and helps her to her feet and then looks at the kitchen door as if to remind her that he likes a snack at twelve. Their main meal is at three o'clock sharp. He then sleeps till five thirty. They have cocktails—or these days an ouzo—at six thirty, after which he retreats to his study till eight. When he comes out, he expects the mahogany table in the main room to be laid with his dinner. Sometimes they watch the television around nine but more often, he returns to his study or goes out, where to she does not know. They go to bed at eleven, which is early for Greece in the summer months. They always get up at six.

Toula has very little to fill her days with. A girl comes twice a week, on Saturdays and Thursdays, to clean 'properly,' as Apostolis says. Toula wipes a wet duster over the furniture on the other days. The meat and fish for the week arrives on Monday. She lowers the basket from the side balcony and the butcher's boy fills it with her order. The fisherman only comes if he has caught *barbounia* – red mullet. Apostolis likes barbounia. The laundry is collected on Tuesdays using the same basket. Up and down it goes on its little electric winch. On Wednesdays, a friend's daughter makes a trip to the *laiki*, the farmer's market, delighting in loading everything into the basket. On Fridays, the laundry comes back clean and ironed.

Taking lettuce and tomatoes from the fridge and a chopping board from the cupboard, Toula begins to make a salad. Two plates are laid before the clocks all wind and grind to their conclusions.

The yellow wooden-legged, formica-topped table adds colour to the kitchen and it may be fifty years old now, but Toula loves it for its sunny colour. She used to bake at this table back when they still lived in the village, her children covered in flour, next door's children running in and out to see if the biscuits were done yet. Then later, sitting at that same table, accounting books spread before her until the early hours of the morning. Apostolis was so grateful at first, before he got involved with that George.

'Here.' Apostolis breaks her reverie as he sits down and throws a letter onto her side plate.

'Oh, who's it from?' Toula looks around for her reading glasses.

'How would I know?' He tears at the bread. His transition has been from village boy to city boy but at moments like this, he plays the role of the village boy again. Only he exaggerates, accentuates the coarseness in his acting. He is untouchable behind his veneer.

Glasses found, Toula examines the postmark.

'Didn't you see it was from England? Surely you know your own daughter's writing?'

'I saw your name and paid it no more attention.' His tone is condescending. 'Do we not have any olives?'

Toula jumps from her seat, feels ever so slightly dizzy and pauses, gripping the edge of the table, her head shaking side to side. When the world steadies, she goes to the cupboard and returns with a glass jar, which she puts on the table unopened. She does not have the strength these days to lever the jars open.

Apostolis takes the jar and grips it between his knees to open it. His strength has faded over the last few years, too. His shirts hang loose and his belts are all done up on the last hole, the muscles of his youth long gone and even the bulk of his successful middle age withered away. She tears the letter open with a crooked finger.

'Look, it's a card! Oh, and Katerina has signed her name, look! We are invited to her third birthday party. Oh my goodness, three already. Darling, can we go? It would be so nice to see where they live, watch Katerina's little face as she opens her present, and we would meet little Apostolis, your namesake, before he is one. Do let's go?' Toula stands and goes through to the sitting room and takes a silver-framed photograph from the writing desk and returns with it. The writing desk belonged to Apostolis' baba. It is the writing desk that he grew up with in the village. Why does he gather these things around him when, in his business dealings, he makes such a big point of creating space between him and his roots?

She puts the framed picture of Apostolis the younger, in his mother's arms in a hospital bed, on the table by the olives and sits down again. Her husband does not answer. He doesn't need to answer; she knows what he will say. There will be unconvincing excuses. He will give reasons why it is not possible just at the moment, and he will promise that they will go in the future. The future she has been waiting for since her daughter moved to a place called Homerton, Hackney, London, four years ago.

The names alone sound delicious. So foreign, such promise of new and exciting things. Hackney, Islington, Camden.

'West Minster.'

'What?'

'Big Ben.'

Apostolis gives her a hard stare.

'Don't they sound exciting, these places? Do you remember when we were young and we had a list of places we wanted to see?'

'Yes, but then we grew up and we had work to do.'

'But there is no work now. Why don't we see these places now?'

'Now we are too old.'

It is on the tip of her tongue to say, 'You might be, but I am not.' But it would not be a kind thing to say, so Toula helps herself to more lettuce.

She can hear the crunch of the stalk of the lettuce inside her ears as she chews. The ticking of the clock on the outside. Empty, hollow sounds.

What if she never sees these places? What if one day, she lays dying and all she can think of are the things she has not done? Places she has not been, people she has not met, nothing in her life except running around after Apostolis. Is that it? Is that her destiny?

'Coffee?' Apostolis requests and takes the picture of their unmet grandchild and puts it back in the front room. Lines it up with the corner of the desk, parallel to the one of his dead mama.

# Juliet

'So you have been back a week already.' Juliet tugs on the handbrake. With her eyes screwed up against the sun, it is possible to see through her dusty windscreen that there is only one yacht in the harbour now. Climbing from behind the steering wheel out of the car and back into the heat, the first noticeable sound is the yacht's halyard clacking against the mast. The boat's hull is a dirty white and there are towels and clothes hanging on the wire handrail between the stantions. An orange beach towel hangs limply over the boom. It has all the appearances of a boat that is someone's home, not a holiday experience. Schools of tiny fish nibble seaweed from a rope that trails loosely in the water from a bollard on the quay. The fisherman's boat is not there.

'I know, life is just spinning past.' Michelle unfolds out of the car and stretches. 'I'm glad I've finished cleaning the house though. It feels my own again now.'

'It doesn't seem like a week since I picked you up from the bus station.'

'It would if you had spent the week cleaning,' Michelle laughs.

'Nor does it seem like a week since I met Toula.' Juliet picks her books off the back seat and pushes them under her arm before they set off. An English Encyclopaedia, a Greek to English dictionary, an exercise book with a pen clipped on its cover.

'Do you know what Marina from the corner shop in the village told me?' Michelle asks as they walk side by side. 'She said she grew up with Toula, knew her before her husband started his construction business. Do you know he started it with a loan that he got from the bank that was meant to be used to extend his house? All a bit naughty, from what I heard.' Michelle's bob needs a trim if she is going to keep it in that style. It is a long time since Juliet has seen it this long. The dress Michelle bought is very similar to her own; light linen, no need to iron.

They walk side by side with long, easy strides until they come to stop by the side of the road, waiting for what little traffic there is to pass.

'Well, this is Greece. The law is not exactly black and white. Even worse in the old days, they say.'

'He deals in clocks now.' Michelle steps out after the last car passes.

'Do you want to stay in town for lunch today?' Juliet asks, hitching up the sinking books.

'We could do. I am going to leave you here and I'll see you in an hour.' Michelle hops onto the pavement at the other side and turns towards the harbour-front cafés.

'You've dropped something.' Juliet bends to pick it up but Michelle is too quick. 'Michelle, that is a military envelope!!'

'So?'

'It's from him isn't it? It's from Dino,' Juliet teases but her eyes are wide, asking for information.

'See you in an hour.'

Juliet watches Michelle's outline become unclear in the glare of the sun. There is just the slightest of squeezes around her heart. She is not sure whether it is heartache from the potential loss of her friend. Maybe she is ready to find someone herself. Maybe the tightness is just a trace of loneliness. The idea of love is very seductive. But there are always complications.

As Juliet passes Toula's door, she can hear clanking and whirring. An involuntary shiver runs the length of her spine and she shakes it off, putting it down to the sudden shade and the sneaky breeze from the north. Soon, she will have to carry around a cardigan or a light jacket. And then a coat in a couple of months as January and February bring the colder weather down from Russia. She will order wood early this year, pay a little more and get the kind that does not spit and burn holes in her rug. A big wood fire with the sofa pulled close and she will remain unmoved until the delicate flowers of spring come to life. If she wanted cold and damp, she would have stayed in England. The cat on Toula's doorstep lifts its head as she passes.

Thoughts of England bring a slight yearning for her boys. Not boys, men! Thomas married now and Terrance, ah Terrance. Will Terrance ever settle down?

There is a couple sitting under the vines at the café, but the other table is free. Juliet makes herself comfortable. When she looks up, Toula is outside her front door, waiting for something or someone. The cat is rubbing itself against the doorframe, making closing the door difficult. Eventually, it slinks into the sunlight to exchange its rubbing post for Toula's legs, making it possible for her to lock the door. She then begins her steady walk towards the café. Her rolling gait already seems familiar. Toula goes into the electrician's as she did last week and comes out again after a minute or two. She picks a sprig of bougainvillea and her smile lights up the street as she draws near.

'Hello *Daskala*,' Toula says, half-English half-Greek. 'Or perhaps I say, "*Kalimera* Teacher?"' Half-Greek, half-English this time. With a glint in her eye, she invites Juliet to enjoy her play.

'How has your week been?' Juliet asks as they order coffees. Toula hesitates and speaks quickly to the waiter in Greek. Juliet understands all that is said. Toula has ordered *loukoumades* and two spoons.

'My week is the same,' she says, exhaling and deflating into the chair. Straightening again, she puts the bougainvillea into the toothpick holder. Juliet moves her chair a fraction so the vine shades her eyes.

'The *electrologos* no come, the lift no good. Apostolis goes his friend George *stin Athina*, again. George is the architect—my husband's business partner.' These two words that she has heard so often in her life roll off her tongue almost without an accent. 'Now George find buyers for clocks. Apostolis buy and sell clocks now. I stay here, alone. My granddaughter, Katerina, is three.' She smiles as if pleased with her long speech.

'George in Athens,' Juliet says.

'That is what I say, George in Athens.'

Juliet wonders whether to press the point. It is not that her student does not know the words in English, it was only a slip. But then, isn't that what these lessons are for?

'Yes, that is what you said, but it came out as "stin Athina,"' Juliet says.

'Oh did I?' Toula is watching the couple on the next table.

'So your granddaughter is three.' Talking about children and grandchildren is always a good way to get pupils to engage. In fact, the most engaging topics for the Greek women she has taught are family, cooking, and cleaning, in that order. With the men, it is politics, women, and gossip, judging by the few she has taught. She moves her chair again. The sun is almost at its height. At least the intense heat of August has passed now.

'Yes, we had invitations to come to her birthday celebrations in London.' There is a sadness in Toula's eye and she takes a hanky from her bag.

'*Eisai endaxi*?' Surprised at the sudden tears and with genuine concern, Juliet asks the question in Greek. Toula's tears colour her sky-blue silk handkerchief the colour of night, the crinkled and parched material greedily soaking the saline.

'Yes, yes,' Toula answers in English, obviously determined to keep the English lesson going. 'It is sad that I cannot go.'

'Why can you not go? What would have happened if you were to go?' Juliet asks. It is another chance to hear Toula's command of the past participle and maybe her future perfect tense.

'It is Apostolis. He does not want to go.' The hanky dabs away at her eyes.

'Go alone?' The words come out before Juliet is aware that she has thought them. They are a reaction to years of being told what she could and could not do by her own husband. Ex-husband. Biting her bottom lip, she wishes she could retract what she has said, or soften the words, make them part of the lesson. But the words are out, and there is no taking them back.

'Alone?' Toula sounds incredulous. Her fingers seek the soft petal of the bougainvillea in the toothpick holder. Her gaze is down the street to her own house, or maybe beyond. Her head begins to shake just a little, side to side as if her neck is loose. Juliet finds she needs to move her chair yet again so she can see Toula's face without being blinded by the sun. From this point of view, it is not the best place for a café.

'Tell me in future tense what you would like to do if you went alone,' Juliet suggests, trying to redeem herself as a teacher.

'Alone?' Toula repeats as if the idea is unthinkable.

Juliet should know better. She has lived in Greece long enough to know that women of Toula's age do nothing alone. They were born into a patriarchal system, raised to be supportive, and encouraged to focus on keeping house and raising children. Travelling abroad is unthinkable. If she goes anywhere without her husband, it will be on a church outing, organised by the *papas*.

'I would go the Big Ben,' Toula says suddenly. Her fingers release the petals and her eyes shine as she looks into Juliet's. 'Westminster! London Bridge, London Tower!'

Juliet nods in encouragement as Toula winds her tongue around these foreign names.

'I would go,' a little knot of muscles appears between her pale eyebrows as she concentrates on the grammar before exploding with, 'Speaker's Corner.' She looks at Juliet for some reaction to these words. 'Speak! Me! Me speak!' The waiter comes out and glances up and down the road, takes a cigarette from behind his ear and, lighting it, ambles to the other side of the narrow road to lean against the building. He stands and smokes, looks up and down the lane. He has an easy grace, as if he is satisfied with his world.

'What would you say?' Juliet is intrigued by this outburst. But Toula now blushes and looks down at her hands in her lap. For a moment, she was free and it was exciting to witness, but now Toula is back in her reality. England has so much to offer women from that point of view, Juliet reflects. The temptation to encourage Toula to follow this dream is great, but Juliet knows this is not her place.

'You do this?' Toula's voice is quiet now, her eyes still fixed on her own knees.

'I do what?' Juliet asks.

'You come the Greece, alone.'

'Yes. I have done this.' Juliet corrects Toula's phrasing as she pushes herself back in her chair, sitting up straighter. She is proud that she came here alone. There was no Michelle here to greet her. She was the first English person in the village. She knew no one. 'Yes I did.'

'Not to be alone? You find a partner easy. A good one. I know, good for you. Clever. How you say. Charms. No, charmings. My nephew mine.'

Juliet's mouth has dropped open, and she shuts it abruptly. She cannot pretend to be surprised. Time and time again, the Greek women do not believe that she chooses to be alone. They are always matchmaking, trying to find someone suitable.

'Er thank you, Toula, but…' She begins but Toula cuts her off.

'Did you have fear, when you come—alone?' Toula moves her own chair, as the sun's progress is now in her face. Her eyes half-close but Juliet can feel the intensity of her stare.

'Was I scared when I came alone? Yes, very. But more than scared, I was angry. Angry at being told what to do with my life all the time by everyone. So the anger outweighed the fear.'

'Out-weighed?' Toula asks for clarification.

'Outweighed. This means the anger was greater than the fear. Its weight was outside the weight of the fear. It weighed more. Do you know any of these phrases, out-run, out-law, out-strip, out-distance?'

'Out-law! Western films.' Toula takes the first sip of her coffee, sucking it quietly through the bubbles on the surface.

'So either it means outside-of, like outside of the law or outside of the number, as in weight.'

'Yes, yes, I see, but I am more thinking about the anger being more than the fear.'

'Oh!' Juliet is not sure what to say and so she takes a drink of her cold coffee. The ice is melting fast. It is sweeter than it was last time, but she is not complaining. The waiter, who had been resting his bottom against the wall, pushes off, glances a smile at Juliet, and returns indoors only to reappear with a plate of *loukomades* with two spoons, which he puts on their table. The couple at the other table pay and leave. There is a sound of voices. The waiter slips back in through the open doors and Juliet becomes aware that there are people drinking coffee inside, too.

'I am angry,' Toula says calmly and the dripping dough ball that Juliet has just scooped onto her spoon falls back into the honey sauce. 'I am angry that he does not keep his promises of places he said we would go. I am angry that he squeeze me out of the business until I am only a housewife. I am angry that the clocks do not all sing at the same time. I am angry that it is good for him to go to stay with George in Athens.' She emphasises these last two words as if to tell Juliet that she has taken on board what was said earlier about her slip back into Greek. 'Whenever he feels like it. But I am meant to stay at home. I am angry that I am not supposed to be angry. This is what I would say at the Speakers Corner.'

Juliet closes her mouth and puts down her spoon to give Toula her full concentration.

# Toula

The anger bubbles. It is a bit like excitement but there is tension in the sinews of her neck, along with a feeling of power. It is not power over anyone, like the power she had over her children until they were of an age to govern themselves, but a power as if she can determine her own future.

'Are you alright?' She can hear Juliet speak but her voice seems a long way away as she looks back towards her house.

How many times has she walked down this street? How many times has she looked at her house? But now it is different, the colours are more intense, heightened, the shadows deeper.

The cat that has recently befriended her is lying on top of an air-conditioning unit by one of the tavernas. It is black with one white paw and long black whiskers. Its coat is sleek, courtesy, no doubt, of the fish tavernas and the many kind strokes of the tourists and the town's residents. It is one of many strays but it is nice the way it has adopted her for the moment. It is a shame Apostolis objects so much to it coming into the house. In truth, she is a little envious of the cat. It can get up and walk away any time it likes. It can move to another street, or find another old lady. It can feed at one taverna or another. It can befriend whom it likes, stay out as long as it likes, and go where it likes. Even a stray cat has more freedom than she has.

She sighs.

But who is really holding her back? If a cat can have this freedom, if Juliet can break free from her old life, then so can she, can't she?

'I go.' Her head quivers on her neck and she has no control but she doesn't care who sees it.

'Do you not want to finish the lesson?' Juliet seems shocked.

'No! You no understand. I go England. Alone. See Katerina, her three birthday.'

'Oh.'

'I go Big Ben, I go Speakers Corner. I go and I want stay.'

'I *will* go to see Big Ben and I *will* go to Speakers Corner and I *will* want to stay.'

Toula cannot really take in Juliet's corrections with this strange churning inside. Her stomach seems to be turning over and her chest feels like it is quivering inside, but she is not cold. A tension around her temples beats with her heart and her breath comes in short gasps. But she feels light, as if she could dance. Right now, if she never sets foot back into that house, with its shutters all closed up against the sun and the perpetual ticking in every corner, sealed to the world outside as time passes, she would not care! In fact, she would celebrate.

Picking up a spoon, she chases a honey-covered ball of pastry around the plate and when it is caught, she opens her mouth and eats in it one, whole. How many times did her own mama scold her for such behaviour? How many times has she refrained from such behaviour in front of Apostolis in fear of his disdain? Well, she is not a child any more and no one should be able to intimidate her and tell her what to do.

She chews contentedly.

'If you say "I go," it implies you are doing it in the now, but if you say "I *will* go," it implies a future action. One that hasn't taken place yet. There is still the possibility that it might not happen. Whereas "I go" is a done deal, as they say. A completed decision,' Juliet explains.

A 'done deal.' That's a good phrase. When they sold the houses that Apostolis built, he would say to her, as she worked on the budgeting of the next build, 'Never count on the money of the last sale until it is in the bank. The deal is not complete until the transfer is done.'

'So I say it right.' Her voice comes through the half-chewed honey ball. 'I go to Big Ben, I go to Speakers Corner, it is done-deal!' The laughter under her ribs escapes as a chuckle, her head wobbling away by itself. Even her hands have a little tremor to them as she lifts another honey ball to her lips. 'You must be quick if you want some of this, Juliet.' She pushes the dish towards her teacher.

Juliet closes her mouth and picks up her spoon.

Taking a paper napkin from the holder that is behind the bougainvillea in the toothpick holder, Toula wipes her mouth. Things like honey get caught in the creases above her lips these days, and in the downward fold in the corners of her mouth. But she is smiling so much as she wipes that the paper touches her teeth, drying them, making her lips stick and the whole process becomes lot more complicated than usual. When she is satisfied she is not dribbling like an old woman she says, 'So Juliet, my teacher, we change lessons.' The sun is in her face again, the cat—her cat—on the air-conditioning unit jumps down and slinks his way towards them, his white paw crossing over the path of his black paw, accentuating the litheness that all the animals have at this time of year. It is the result of a month of such intense heat. He stops and shakes, creating a cloud of

49

dry dust, out of which he walks with an arrogant attitude.

'Lessons every day now. My English more-better *out-weighs* everything else.'

She must go to the travel agents, arrange tickets. Yes, she can manage that. Call her daughter to tell her she is coming. It will be good to talk to her, maybe it will cement her plans, give her confidence. She must also go into the guest room and take out her winter clothes. It will be so much colder in London. Is all this for real? Is she really planning to go to London? How would Apostolis survive? A naughty voice in her head says she doesn't care if he survives or not, but the truth is it will be no difficulty for her to arrange for the shops to deliver groceries as usual or maybe… Yes, this is even better: when she goes, Apostolis can stay with George in Athens.

It feels unreal and at the same time more real than anything she has ever done in her life. Her surety comes in equal measures to her overwhelming terror, the two oscillating, pulling her up, pushing her down. The thoughts make her head spin.

'I know we say *pio poli* in Greek, but in English, "more-better" is considered wrong. Use one or the other, but in this case, you don't need

50

either. It makes sense if you just say that your need to learn English outweighs everything else.'

But Toula can only think of making lists in her head.

'Hi guys. Am I too early?' They both turn their heads as Michelle comes up to their table.

Toula looks at her watch. 'Oh, the time is like bird, as the English say.'

'Time has flown,' Juliet corrects, but Toula is not listening.

'Tomorrow, same time.' It is not a question. Toula points to her watch.

'Oh, okay. Yes, if you are serious.' Juliet smiles but she is also frowning.

Toula does not answer. Instead, she gives Juliet her sternest look. She has never been more serious. After Apostolis has eaten his lunch and he goes into his study, she will slip out again and go to the travel agents. Hopefully, they will not close in the heat of the afternoon like some shops do. Then she can buy her ticket.

# Juliet

Juliet watches Toula go.

'Good lesson?' Michelle asks.

'Yes. No. Not sure.' Juliet uncoils herself, stretching her legs out. She hadn't realised she was so tense.

'Why? What happened?'

'It was as if she had some sort of epiphany, suddenly deciding that she was going to go off to England on her own to see her grandchildren.'

'Good for her. A frappe please, *glyko*.' Michelle address the waiter who is standing, staring at Juliet.

'Maybe she just likes the idea that she will go on her own. Maybe she won't follow it through.' Juliet frowns. 'But she has asked me to give her lessons every day until she goes.'

'Are you going to do it?' Michelle leans her shopping bags against the leg of the table.

'I said I would.'

They fall into silence, watching the old woman progress down the lane.

# Toula

Toula stops just before her house to pinch off another sprig of bougainvillea. She will put it in a vase on the yellow kitchen table. The cat is by her feet, its fur so soft. The creature is so friendly. It is nice to have something to love.

As the key turns in the lock, she is deep in thought, trying to imagine what it must be like to live in London and be cold all the time. No doubt the houses are properly insulated with boilers that work, lifts that move, and radiators that do not leak brown water onto the floor to soak between boards and stain the ceiling below.

She has not seen pictures of her daughter's house, not as such. But she has always studied what is in the background of the photographs full of smiles. The living room is in cream, with a white sofa with golden cushions. Katerina's bedroom has a painting on the wall of a forest with birds in bright colours and a deer peeping from behind a tree trunk. The kitchen is modern, with black work surfaces and long, vertical chrome handles on the white cupboards.

Did she remember to pay just now, or has she left Juliet with the bill? She stops as she is putting her weight to the door and tries to remember. No, she did pay. She left a note and some coins on the table next to Juliet's money.

She shoves with her whole weight and the door opens. The cat rushes in ahead of her. Looking up the broad wooden polished stairs, she waits for her eyes to adjust to the relative dark. The lift stopped again a couple of days ago when she was coming down with the heavy rubbish bag from the kitchen. She jumped up and down, the counterweight shifted, the wheel at the top that the big cable loops round gave a quarter turn, and she dropped enough, and quite suddenly, to be able to open the ground floor doors and take a big step down to get out. After putting the rubbish in the bin, she went back up by the stairs. Complaining to Apostolis resulted in him pressing the button a few times. The lift worked for him, and he declared there was nothing wrong.

She will take the stairs today. Her old legs have energy and besides, she does not want to lose this mood she is in by growing cross, or worse, hysterical, about being stuck in the lift. The cat investigates the lift and then springs up the stairs.

The sound of multiple ticking grows louder as Toula nears the top.

The chiming begins as she opens the upper door and without bothering to raise her voice to call out to Apostolis, she goes straight to the kitchen to make his snack. Five minutes later, after she has given the cat half a tin of tuna, they are eating in silence. At one point, she opens her mouth to tell him that she will be booking a ticket, but maybe it would be better if she bought the ticket first. Made it a *fait accompli*, as they say in France.

'French,' she says aloud, helping herself to another thin slice of the feta and spinach pie that she made the night before.

'Pardon?' Apostolis has a tendril of spinach hanging on his chin. He does not look up.

'Nothing. I just thought of a word and it was French.'

'Oh.' He turns the page of the magazine he is reading. He has been subscribing to this magazine about clocks for years. His rule about not reading at the table has never been upheld when his magazine arrives. Toula suspects that if it was her magazine, there would be stern looks and a brief word. But how does he even read them? His English back in school was never very good and he has had no reason to learn since. Only occasionally does she catch him running his finger under the script very slowly.

When he becomes aware of her watching, he stops.

It had better be a *fait accompli*. A done deal, as they say in England. Buy the tickets first. She swallows a mouthful of the thin red wine to stifle her excitement.

After his snack, he retires to his study. His radio, which he always leaves on, is turned up louder than its usual low mumble. His door is open just a crack. Toula decides the bedroom phone would be more private. But in this decision, she becomes uncomfortably aware that she is trying to hide something. It is not a secret, so she does not go upstairs to use the phone. She goes upstairs to take off her earrings, which are pinching a little. It is just coincidence that she decides to call Alyssia whilst she is there.

The bedsprings give as she sits. The cat appears, leaps onto the bed, and curls up on her knee.

'Hello Alyssia?'

'Ella Mama, *ola kala*?'

'I am well.' Toula decides to practice her English.

'How is Baba?' Alyssia switches effortlessly from Greek to English and back again.

'He is as always. I have the card from Katerina.' The cat's fur is so silky and smooth.

'Good, I will tell her. I am sorry you will not be able to come. She would so like it if she saw more of you and Baba, but I guess this is the life we have chosen.' Her laugh is like ice cubes against crystal to Toula's ears. Her spine straightens and she looks far beyond the crack of sunshine between the slats of the pale grey shutters, imagining her beautiful daughter, a woman of the world, living in London.

'So I am not coming?' Toula teases her beloved offspring and rubs the cat's nose.

'Mama, I know how it is with Baba. It's okay. I will explain to Katerina how far away you are. Maybe if you got a computer, we could Skype?'

'Well, I have a surprise to tell you. I am coming!' There, she is committed now. The quivering in her chest grows stronger but the lightness inside her head is wonderful. The cat jumps off.

'What? How did you talk Baba into coming? Really, Mama? That is so wonderful. I will pick you up from the airport, of course. Do you have your times and dates yet? Come for a while, Mama. Do not come just for a few days. A week, no two, at least. How did you manage this with Baba?' Alyssia's intake of breath fills the phone.

'Your Baba, he is not coming. Baba, he does not know yet that I am coming.'

'Oh.' Alyssia's deflation is as noisy as her earlier outburst was. How many times has Toula heard that same sigh as Alyssia grew from a child to the rebellious teenager that she became, over promises made to her and then broken by Apostolis when she was so little. Simple things such as going for a walk, playing ball. Then there were the possibilities she discovered through her friends when at school; ball parks, water parks, dancing lessons, all of which filled her little heart with such joy, only to have a smoothing rug of procrastination thrown over them by Apostolis. The practicalities of going, the procrastination of paying for lessons, the organising of lifts, the scheduling of time—all being put off until it was clear that for her, such things would never be. Over and over, Alyssia had her hopes dashed until she almost had no hope left at all. Her rebelling in her teenage years shocked Apostolis, but Toula understood. She, too, had promises dashed. Promises of travel, of working together, of doing up their village house, spending time together, him not going to Athens so often, leaving her alone, moving back to the village once they were retired, travelling once they were retired, visiting Alyssia in England as well as all the little everyday things he promised and never fulfilled.

Coffee in the square that never happened. Friends round for dinner who were never invited. New shutters that would open that were never ordered. Air conditioning units that never materialised. None of it from a lack of money.

'Alyssia, listen. I am coming.' Toula speaks firmly. 'I, me, your mama, Toula. I am coming. Just me alone. This is not to do with your Baba.'

'Thank you, Mama, but we both know how he is.' Alyssia sounds defeated. The anger within Toula that has been sitting somewhere inside her solar plexus since talking to Juliet rears up and tightens across her chest. It stiffens her jaw and her teeth clench. She is not going to let her daughter down, not now, and not ever again.

'I will tell you how it is. When I close the phone to you and your baba has fallen sleeping, I go to the travel peoples and I take a ticket.' Her English is falling to pieces with the speed she is talking, but she does not care.

'But Mama, how will you get to the airport?'

'The railway line to Corinth is open now, so there is trains all the way. A taxi to take me to the station. It is not difficult.' As she says the words, the anger changes to fear and then back to anger again. She will go. Women her age travel the world over all the time. Thousands have done it before her, and thousands will do it after her. If she can give birth with no help, she can take a plane to London.

'Mama, do you want me to send you some money?'

Toula knows why Alyssia has asked. Ever since Apostolis squeezed her out of their building business after Alyssia was born, even though their wealth was growing, he took tighter and tighter control over the money. All through Alyssia's life, if money was needed, it involved a lengthy explanation to Baba and an account of it once it was spent. Toula explained to Alyssia that it was because they were brought up poor farmers in a rural village but even when she said it, she knew it was not the real truth.

Apostolis liked the control. He still likes the control.

Sure, she gets housekeeping money, but Apostolis collects the receipts. They do have a joint bank account and in theory she can draw money out, but in all their married life, she has never done this.

Perhaps this is something she should do. It would be better to do it now and learn how it is done than wait until a time that forces her to learn.

Kyria Zephyria, from the village, after her husband died, had her electricity cut off before she dared go to the bank and take out some money. How poor Zephyria must have worried. She never said anything at the funeral or any time after. She must have thought she was going to starve to death. All for not knowing what to do and say in the bank.

Toula smooths the bedspread on either side of where she is sitting.

But look at Zephyria now! A new dress every few weeks, her house all tight against the weather and the insects. Double glazing to keep out the heat and the hum of the village. Insulation in the roof to keep the chill out in the winter. Air conditioning in the bedroom to make it possible to sleep in the summer. She lives like a queen since her husband's death. And does she miss him? Not one jot. How easy her life must be.

'Thank you, Alyssia. You have always been a considerate girl, but I will go to the bank and take money out. How is young Apostolis? Tell me he does not look like his pappou?'

The two of them dissolve into laughter and continue to chat about nothing in particular for another half an hour or so. But a small part of Toula's mind is pondering over Apostolis' health. He is getting thinner. Maybe he won't be around too many more years. It would be a mercy if she had some life left to live after he has gone.

# Juliet

The following day, Michelle chooses to come into town with Juliet and as they cross the road, Juliet is reminded of the letter that Michelle had dropped.

'You made a very neat job of avoiding my question yesterday.'

'Which question?' Michelle has a pair of shoes in her hand that she is taking in to be mended. Juliet regrets not bringing hers. It is better to do these things before the weather turns cooler and the cobbler has a sudden influx of winter shoes.

'That letter?' Juliet prompts.

'Ah.' It is a sound that suggests she is not going to say any more.

'Michelle?'

'What?'

'Oh come on. It was from him, wasn't it?' Juliet has an interest not only for Michelle's sake but for young Dino, too. He was just another boy from the village until he fell for her friend. Now Juliet cares for him too.

'Maybe,' Michelle says.

'Do you really expect me not to care or be interested?' Juliet adopts a teasing tone but she cannot keep the edge out of her voice. Michelle

63

can be so frustrating at times. Does she think her life will not be affected if they become a couple?

They turn onto Toula's street. The café is empty and they choose the chairs with the most shade. Michelle puts her shoes on the table and then immediately changes her mind and puts them on the floor, sweeping the dust they leave behind onto the floor with her forearm.

'So, what does he say?' Juliet presses.

Michelle sits back and takes the letter from her bag.

'I'm not sure you are going to approve.'

'Tell me.' She braces herself. She wishes nothing more than for her friend to find happiness and companionship, or even love. This wish for her wellbeing will be enough to cover her feelings, to hide her sadness at possibly being left on her own over the winters.

'Okay.' Michelle pulls out the leaves of thin paper from the envelope. They look well-worn already.

'I just want it to be known,' Michelle provides an introduction with steady eye contact, 'that I have not been in touch with him since he left last autumn. I have given him a chance to realise he is too young to be with me, that he needs to find his own life. I kept my side of the deal.'

'That was a deal you made with yourself, Michelle. No one else put pressure on you.' Juliet has no problem returning her stare.

A pair of legs by her side breaks her concentration.

'Two frappes, one *metrio* and one *glyko*, please.' Michelle mixes the Greek words in with the English to the waiter, who nods and goes inside. Juliet encourages Michelle to read by touching the pages. Michelle is looking after the waiter.

'You know he stares at you?'

'Read,' Juliet commands.

'Just saying. He's nice looking, our age.'

'Michelle!'

'Okay, okay. Dear Michelle.' Michelle clears her throat and moves her chair nearer to Juliet, leaning in towards her, holding the papers closer to her eyes and speaking in hushed tones. She looks up as a man walks past, talking to himself, or rather into a telephone earpiece. He passes unaware of them both and Michelle continues.

'I have tried very hard to do as you asked. To not write to you, to not contact you and to go out and have my own life with people my own age — and I have.'

A tiny gasp escapes Juliet and she looks at Michelle who is stony-faced.

The frappes arrive and Michelle waits until the waiter has gone back inside before progressing.

'After three weeks here, we then had to swear allegiance to Greece. Once we had sworn, we were allowed out on leave. I could have come to you, but I didn't. I did as you suggested. I have been out with groups of friends I have made here in the army, men my own age, or should I say boys. They seem so young. Nice, but young. They have lived such easy lives. Whilst on leave with them, I have met their sisters and their friends, girls who are also my own age and they are nice. Some of them are good fun, some even educated, but there is something (and forgive me if you find this word harsh but I can think of no better word in English), insipid (is that how you spell it?) about their characters and they cannot hold my attention for long.'

Michelle stops to look at Juliet who, as she takes a sip of her drink, is eager to hear more and points at the letter to indicate that Michelle should continue.

'I can honestly say I have tried. I have done as you ask, as you requested. I did it wholeheartedly with the intention of trying to forget you. It has been many months since I have

66

seen you, coming up to a year now, and I am writing to you now to tell you that your method has failed. My feelings have not changed. If anything, they have grown stronger and I repeat again: Michelle, will you marry me?'

Juliet explodes with a tight chortle and then smiles and pats Michelle's knee. Michelle ignores her and continues.

'I have eight months left to serve. I know nothing of your life since we parted. Did you manage to sell your house in England for the price that would allow you to buy that small hotel on Orino and the barn next to Juliet's? If so, have you made the barn so you can live in it? Or has none of this happened? Have you moved back to England and continued your life without me?

'My only connection to you is this mailing address. I can only hope they are forwarding your mail. If I hear nothing from you, I will write to Juliet. I feel sure she would forward my letters to you.'

Juliet nods as if Dino is present, assuring him that she would.

'If, for whatever reasons, you have returned to England, I want to tell you that when I am released, I will follow. Whatever it takes, I am prepared to give.

Please write to me. Let me know that you have received it.

'With a heart full of love,'

Michelle mutters these words.

'Dino.'

'Oh my, oh my,' Juliet says and with a big sniff, she throws her head back and looks at Michelle, who is still looking at the letter, her face unreadable. Two women walk past, arms linked, strolling in the heat, heads bent in to one another, talking quietly.

'So, and I quote, "If he asks to marry me again in six months, I will take him seriously." So now you must take him seriously, what are you going to do?'

Michelle says nothing.

'How do you feel towards him? Do you want to be with him? Do you still feel the same as you did last summer or has all that emotion gained some perspective?' Juliet waits as Michelle considers her reply.

'No.' Michelle says emphatically and takes a suck on her straw. Her face muscles are tight, her grip on the glass turning her knuckles white. Juliet waits.

'No, the emotion has not gained any perspective, as you put it. I yearn for him.' She pulls a face as she says the word *yearn*. It is overly passionate for Michelle's usual vocabulary. 'But I have to question myself; am I yearning for the child I never had? Or am I wishing for a time that is now passed, wishing back my youth that never was because it was all exams and studying?'

'Or are you over complicating it and thinking too much? I remember a time when you told me I was doing something like that. Maybe you just love him.'

'When he reaches forty and wants a shiny, red racing car and a young Barbie girl on his arm, I will be sixty-five.' Michelle speaks as if these are thoughts she has had a hundred times, and Juliet suspects that is probably the case. But she knows from experience that once she gives in to emotion, it is almost impossible to reason feelings away with logic.

Michelle's mouth is a tight line, and she is looking anywhere but at Juliet.

'Yes, you are right,' Juliet states emphatically. 'Better to not have his love now in case that happens in the future.' She nods sagely, leans back, and uncrosses her ankles.

'Says you, Mrs Too-Scared-To-Have-Any-Relationship-At-All!'

'Get lost.' Juliet says it as a joke. It is the sort of phrase they used to address each other when they were teenagers, but she can hear the edge in her voice. She smiles to soften the words. Michelle has her lawyer's gaze fixed on her now. She bets Michelle must have been really good in her wig and gown before she gave it all up for her life over here.

They drink their coffees in silence.

'So, what are you going to do?' Juliet asks again, when enough time has elapsed to take the focus off her last words.

'I bought a postcard to write back. I was just going to write a line or two; I don't want to be rude. But then I thought a postcard in return for his heartfelt words would be giving him short change.'

'That's a slight understatement. So what are you going to do?' Juliet can see Toula coming out of her door, the cat by her ankles. Her conversation with Michelle is going to have to wait.

'So I am going to the cobblers. Here comes Toula!' Michelle's words are packed with relief. The subject shelved; she is off the hook.

'We'll get some wine afterwards and go back and sit in the garden and drink to Dino's health.' Michelle rolls her eyes, but her mouth betrays a smile. When they drink wine together, it usually becomes rowdy, laughing and carrying on like teenagers again at first and then melancholy as the wine digs deeper and they sort out all the troubles in the world. Invariably, they are left with hangovers but also in a better place, clearer about their lives, however painful that may or may not be.

'Hello,' Toula greets them both.

'Hello Toula, and goodbye, Toula. I am off to the cobblers.' Michelle waves the shoes to demonstrate.

'Ah, cobblers. *Tsangaris*?' Toula asks.

'Yes. Cobblers. *Tsangaris*,' Juliet says and gives Michelle one last glance as she walks away.

# Toula

'So I go!' Toula announces. It is good to see Juliet. Something about her endorses this new courage she has found. Yesterday, as Apostolis slept, her courage faltered and she felt like she was forcing herself to go to the travel agents. It is a narrow shop wedged between a betting shop full of idle or desperate men and a haberdashery where she buys her underwear. She had never been in before. The bell over the door tinkled as she entered. On the walls, posters were curling off, faded by the bright sun. Behind a computer, a girl sat, talking on the phone, and looking bored. One or two brochures were arranged on a small coffee table in what looked like a waiting area but as there was no one else, there was no need to wait.

The girl put the phone down immediately and was most helpful. Toula had quite liked her right up until the point when she asked when Kyrios Apostolis would call in to pay for the tickets. Yes, tickets, not ticket! She presumed he was going with her! The same sort of thing happened in the bank where she went to learn how to draw out the money to pay for that ticket. The cashier did not actually ask Toula

72

where her husband was, but her momentary look of panic said it all.

So twice Toula felt she had been challenged, and twice she had had to stand up for herself. But the interesting thing was that each time, even though it annoyed her, the experience didn't undermine her confidence, which is what she would have expected. In fact, the challenges had the effect of making her more determined, more adamant. When she arrived home with not only a ticket but also a handful of English ten pound notes, she found Apostolis sitting in the main room, pretending to read past copies of his magazines. He was clearly waiting for her.

The clocks started to chime six o'clock as he opened his mouth. It was a good few minutes before they all rung their last and the resonance stopped echoing around the panelled walls and wooden floors. This gave her additional time in which to brace herself, but she found she was remarkably calm.

'I have just had a call from the bank manager,' he began. He put last November's edition of the magazine down carefully. He had clearly decided what he wanted to say and was gathering his thoughts for the first words, his lips and tongue moving into position. Toula surprised herself. She cut him off as he uttered his first sound.

'Lovely man, the bank manager. My friend Zephyria, from the village, is his first cousin. He also proved very helpful. I needed to withdraw some money, as I have decided to accept Katerina's invitation to her birthday party.' Toula could not tell if it was excitement or fear she felt, but now that she was speaking, it was probably best to finish the whole job. 'I think whilst I am away, maybe the best thing is that you go and stay with George in Athens.'

The look on his face was worth savouring. But then he closed his mouth. With a laboured intake of breath through his nose, he appeared ready to reply. At this point, Toula spoke out again.

'We can take the same train up if you like. You can jump out at Iraklio and take the metro from there and I will continue to the airport.' She did not wait for his reply with this announcement. Instead, she went upstairs and started packing her bag. But once out of the room, she exhaled loudly, paused to stop herself shaking, and then set out on a mission to unearth her winter coat. She would need it at this time of year in England. The cat appeared from nowhere, upstairs in her bedroom! Her immediate response was to worry about what Apostolis would say if he saw the little furry mite there. She should shoo it away, but this thought was overpowered by her need to cuddle the soft, warm bundle. It didn't object. Clutching it in her arms, she even buried her face in its smooth fur, breathing in the clean cat smell. How easy it is to fall in love with an animal. It purred its thank you, eyes narrowed, definitely smiling.

Lost in the exchange of love, a good ten minutes passed before she resumed her selection of clothes she would need. The cat helped by lying in her suitcase.

Her head wobbled and quivered and her hands shook as she packed. The laying out of her clothes felt like she was breaking some unwritten rule. She knew that if Apostolis came in at this moment, her nerve might fail. Focusing on the job in hand and stroking the cat stopped her stomach churning. She would take the larger suitcase so she could also pack some bottles of olive oil and jars of preserves. Maybe even a box of *baklava* from the *zacharoplasteio*.

'To England?' Juliet's question bring her back to the present.

'Yes. I buy ticket. I have English pound. I phone my daughter, she come the airport on London. I go! The two weeks.' The excitement is gripping her again.

'You will be going in two weeks' time.' Juliet reiterates what she has said, presumably to correct her grammar, but it is Juliet who has it wrong.

'No, I go two weeks. I leave tomorrow!' Toula cannot help beaming. Katerina will crawl all over her, little hands grabbing at her clothes for balance as she wriggles to sit on her knee. They will smoother each other with kisses. Then there is baby Apostolis, who she will hold for the first time. She feels quite dizzy with excitement.

'Tomorrow!' Juliet sounds so enthusiastic. Always so enthusiastic, it is her manner. She will have more lessons when she comes back, just to spend time with someone so positive. She would like to get to know Juliet's friend, too.

'You are a woman of action!' Juliet adds.

'A woman of action.' Toula says the words in her head. She likes the label and wonders if it could be true? But she almost feels as if her action was pressed upon her. After Apostolis went to lie down, her initial impetus wavered. The idea of going to England felt unreal. With thought, it became nothing more than a fantasy.

That was when she received a call from her friend Zephyria in the village. Her weekly call for a chat, about this and that, nothing in particular. Zephyria, who sounded so strong and confident now, but it was not long ago that she had been forced to face her own insecurities.

'You know what I thought? I thought of my friend Zephyria. Maybe you know her? She lives in the village.' Juliet shakes her head slightly as if she is not sure if she knows Zephyria or not.

'Well, Zephyria did not know how to run her life after her husband died. The practical side of life was such a shock to her. She didn't know even that they had money in the bank, let alone how to get it, or how to pay bills. She knew nothing! They even cut off her electricity because she did not know how to take money from one place and put it in another. She had been surviving on the coins in the jar on the mantelpiece, each week buying less and less food as it ran out. When someone finally saw she needs help, she had not eaten for a day and was burning candles in the evenings.'

'Oh yes, I heard about her.' But Juliet says no more. She gives the impression of not being one to gossip. But this is important. It does not feel like gossip to explain what she learnt from Zephyria's mistakes.

'Well, I decide I did not want to suffer like Zephyria if Apostolis dies before me, which he will. He is older and he is a man. So I decide it would be better to learn how to take money from the bank now. Do things by myself before he dies. It is not only his money. I have lived by his side, started the business, raised his children, kept his house!'

'Absolutely,' Juliet replies. More proof of what a positive person she is.

'Only...' Toula slumps in her chair. The bougainvillea she put in the toothpick holder when she arrived looks a little silly all of a sudden. Like she is trying to make something pretty when it isn't. It is a stainless steel toothpick holder, ugly in shape and sterile in nature. It is something she has been accused of all her life. Living in a fantasy world, her mama used to say. *Only seeing what you wants to see*, Apostolis had observed more than once. Does her bougainvillea in the toothpick holder just serve to illustrate more clearly that this is her nature?

Is that what she is doing with all this rushing about? Is this sudden play at being independent just a distraction, a huge bouquet of bougainvillea that she is focusing on so she can ignore what is really going on, to ignore her true feelings?

The world swims behind filmy eyes. These thoughts are not comfortable; she has not requested them! Apostolis was so crushing. He came up when she had nearly finished packing. The cat slithered off the bed and made a sly exit before it was spotted. Apostolis watched her smooth out her blouses and push rolled-up pairs of woolly tights down the sides of the case for a while before he spoke.

That was the wrong coat to take, he said. She would need heavier shoes, he informed her. How would she find her way from the aeroplane to where Alyssia was meeting her? Had she told Alyssia that she was abandoning him? He would like to see her telling Katerina that she had left him without anyone to care for him.

But it was the way he said these things, as if she had committed the greatest crime the world had ever known. All the time he was speaking in his sad and quiet little voice, he adjusted an oil painting here, a marble statue there as if to emphasis the rich life he had given her. The tension in the room was thick and oppressive. But she did not back down. She kept packing — what else could she do — until he eventually went away. Then she sat on the bed and sobbed. The cat jumped onto her lap.

He started again at dinner. Making food was her job, always had been. She was abandoning her post. He was trying to stir up feelings of guilt. The same when it was time for bed. Where were his pyjamas? That almost made her laugh—but in a very unkind way. She has done neither the washing nor the ironing since they moved to Saros. The dry cleaners come to the house, have done for years, as do the butcher, the baker, and the vegetable man. Everyone comes to them. The rich Maraveyas.

Laundry is on a Tuesday. Every Tuesday she lowers the washing in a basket from the balcony to the boy who waits on his moped, and on a Friday he beeps his horn twice and she levers the washing back up. This is the balcony round the side of the house, where she planted a fig tree in a pot when they first moved in. It has now grown so large and heavy that the marble balcony has cracked.

Apostolis had a small and very ugly winch attached to the wall on this balcony so his mother could have this job when she was alive. Toula complained about its ugliness at the time, but now she no longer cares what it looks like. It is her godsend now.

But, as Apostolis well knows, once the washing is back in the house, she never puts the clothes away. The girl who comes in twice a week to clean does that, and she always puts everything in the same place. He was just trying to pin another job on her so he could suggest she was not fulfilling her role. More guilt.

She stifled her bitter laugh and ignored his question, going to the bathroom to put her teeth to soak. When she returned, he had his pyjamas on. He knew exactly where to find them.


'Yes, better I learn to do all things before he dies, only…'

'Only what?' Juliet asks.

'Can I tell you something in secret, Juliet?' Toula blinks away her tears.

'Well, I…'

But it must be said.

'Now I have taken money from the bank and bought the ticket to London, I am independent. I say him he will stay with his friend George in Athens when I am away and that we will take the train up to Athens together. I say him.' She pauses. 'He did not say me! Before this, I blame my unhappiness on having to do as I was told, like a childs. But now I am not doing what I am told, I can see that my unhappiness is in my hands. I now feel I have enough to be able to say to myself that I am not, how you say, *ikanopiimeni*,'

'Content,' Juliet translates.

'Yes, content. I am not this, and here is the secret.' She leans in closer, catching the light, flowery smell of Juliet's perfume. 'I want to be free of him.' Just the words alone taste delicious on her tongue.

She exhales. Saying these words that she has dreamed, felt, and until now has only thought, increases the weight she feels is pulling her down. It gives her no relief. She picks up the bougainvillea from the toothpick holder and studies it more closely. From a distance, the flower appears to be made up of coloured petals but close up, they are definitely leaves. Hardy somehow, rougher than the tiny white flowers, whilst also translucent. Beautiful from a distance but always a bit of a con on closer scrutiny.

# Juliet

Juliet shivers. It runs the length of her spine, as it did the first day she saw Toula. There is something so deeply sad about the old lady and yet when she smiles, the whole world lights up. Her confession about wanting to be rid of her husband has not shocked Juliet. Too many marriages are arranged when both parties are too young, sometimes for the sake of land, or out of some other convenience. It has been the way in rural Greece for as long as anyone can remember.

Just the other day, Juliet congratulated her dentist on her marriage, only to be rewarded with a half smile.

'What, don't you love him?' Juliet teased, a giggle ready. Her cheerfulness to cover her nerves, totally confident that her dentist would reply that of course she loves her fiancé. This was a successful woman, who had studied in Athens and was bilingual, modern.

'No,' came the stark reply. Lost for what to say, Juliet asked, 'Does he love you?'

'No.' The second reply. 'But it will be secure, for both our families.' Even though these lives do not touch upon her own, the harsh reality hurt Juliet more than the drilling. So sad.

Traditionally, these arranged marriages work well. The women tend house and, on many occasions, love grows over the years and the couples are happy. Maybe she should not judge. But with Toula, the balance does not seem right. She has very little force, she is so soft, so gentle that it is all too easy to imagine her husband, whom Juliet has not met but knows by reputation, could easily and perhaps unknowingly bully her.

Juliet shakes her head as if to clear her mind. Relationships, love, it is the one theme that seems to cause as much harm as good.

Toula, on the one hand, is thinking hard about herself and consequently thinks she wants to be rid of her husband. Michelle, on the other hand, is thinking hard on behalf of Dino and thinks he should want to be rid of her for his own sake.

The whole dating, mating thing is too complex, with too many pitfalls, too much broken heartache. This is why she has stayed single so long. It is all so time-consuming, energy draining. Maybe a little loneliness is a small price to pay for a consistent life.

As for Toula, maybe two weeks in London will show her a different side of life. London will probably shock her. The question of independence no longer on feminine lips in the city. They live the lives they want and there are laws, now old laws, about discrimination. Emancipated woman of England are now thinking of others who are suppressed. They are the liberators now, largely unaware that it was just fifty years ago, less even, that there was no such thing as equality. Juliet can remember what it used to be like, and she is only fifty-two. Women may have not arrived yet but at least they are moving in the right direction.

With a heavy sigh, Juliet tries to let go of her strong views. Greece has all this liberation still to go through. It will take a generation or two to catch up. At the moment, many of the independent young women of Athens accept the subservient roles of their mamas and yiayias. It is not even only the yiayias and mamas. Just the other day, when Juliet was backing out of a parking spot in Saros, a woman had come driving round the corner at breakneck speed whilst chatting on her mobile and the two cars collided. Juliet's concern was whether the woman was injured. The driver's door opened and a designer knee-length boot appeared first, followed by skinny fit jeans, complete with rhinestones adorning the pocket's edges. The look was completed with a crisp blouse undone

one button too low and designer bling filling the woman's cleavage. Her hair was beautifully maintained and her makeup was immaculate. A modern woman.

'Are you alright?' Juliet inquired. The woman looked fine.

'Yes but...' She looked down at her dented car. 'What is it best that we do now?'

'I'll get my details.' Juliet opened her passenger door and then the glove compartment for her insurance documents.

The woman shifted her weight from one designer heel to the other and when Juliet starting unfolding the official papers, she said, a slight panic in her eyes, 'I think it is best we call our husbands,' in a whispering, breathy voice.

Juliet felt her mouth drop open and she straightened to look the woman in the face, wondering if she was making a joke.

'You have a mobile to call him, or do you want to borrow mine?' the woman said, offering the latest in technology to Juliet.

Toula is trying to jump that gap. Of course she would think she wanted to be free of her husband. For him just not to be around is a far easier option than everyone adjusting their thinking and their way of behaving. She is trying to leap a gap of inequality that is not even completely closed in England—despite what they say. Look at the government in the UK, so biased toward men. All of them come through the same schooling and throughout the UK women still only get paid fifty-eight pence for every pound that men get.

Juliet recognises her thinking has fallen into well-worn grooves. She shakes herself free of these pointless, energy-consuming thoughts.

'Well, you will be free for two weeks!' Juliet decides that it is best to keep her questioning thoughts to herself.

'Yes, I will.' Toula finds her smile again and the rest of the hour passes with much humour. Some of Toula's jokes about Apostolis are a little unkind. But who is Juliet to judge with all the unkind things she said and thought about Mick around the time she got divorced? For a while, she was really quite bitter.

At one point, Toula says again she knows of a man that would suit Juliet so well. Juliet changes the subject.

When Toula leaves, she kisses Juliet a fond farewell on both cheeks. Juliet wishes her *sto kalo*—go to the good. With her head wobbling slightly, Toula's slow, steady pace toward her house seems so familiar now. If Juliet had not split up from Mike when the boys went to University, that might well have been her, a little old lady in a bar-less prison, held by fear of the unknown and lack of self-belief. She is glad that even at this late stage, Toula is thinking about liberating herself.

'If a woman never takes off her high-heeled shoes, how will she ever know how far she can walk or how fast she can run?' Juliet whispers the quote towards the receding Toula, to offer her invisible strength, solidarity.

Her steady steps slow as she reaches the bougainvillea, but then Toula seems to change her mind and continues empty-handed. At her door, she fumbles in her bag, presumably for her key. She seems to take so long, Juliet checks the table, around the coffee cups, to see if any keys have been left behind, but there are none.

Toula's grey head leans in toward the door, but from this distance Juliet cannot hear the words clearly. There is only a murmur and the old lady's lips move.

One time when Juliet found herself in conversation with one of the port police—a radio operator, if memory serves—he told her that the acoustics up and down the stairwells of these old house are strange. If you put your ear to the door at the bottom, apparently, you can hear every word spoken in the apartments above, in the stairwells and, even, if there is one, in the lift shaft. He said that, with the overly zealous captain they had at the time, he and his colleagues had found many an opportunity to eavesdrop before mounting the stairs to the port police office. It had kept them out of a lot of trouble, being able to concoct alibies and excuses before being met at the top of the stairs with accusations and wrath.

Toula's conversation continues until the dark red door suddenly changes to black as it is opened inward. She steps into the shadows and a cat rushes out, panicking for its freedom.

At that moment, a group of teenagers fills the end of the lane and their noise breaks the peace. Their adult bodies are at odds with their juvenile movements and noise. They swarm together, three of them are singing loudly, the boys play-fighting as they walk, and a group of girls, arms linked, walk carefully, aware of their every move on display. Their clothes are brightly coloured, the language loud and flamboyant, their movements full of energy. They walk straight past Juliet's table and the little café as if they did not see it or her. The chairs are bumped into and moved out of the way and they take their life and noise with them further up the street, where they turn a corner and the place falls silent again.

Toula's door is now shut. The cat is climbing onto the air conditioning unit.

Juliet thanks the waiter, who is in no hurry to lose her presence, before she heads in the direction of her car. It is time to go and see Michelle, whom she left chewing on the end of her pen, trying to compose a letter to Dino, lounging by the pool that was installed to attract paying guests to the holiday-let cottage.

The night before, the wine had flowed. Initially, Michelle might as well have had her wig and gown on as she explained why she and Dino could never be together, so carefully and clinically she had outlined her argument. But as the moon rose higher, the bats began their evening swoop over the surface of the swimming pool for insects. Drained glasses were refilled and logic and caution were progressively abandoned until Michelle cried to the stars over her everlasting love for the young Dino. She declared she was only going to live once, so she might as well live to the fullest.

Juliet did her best to make all her comments ambiguous so as not to lead Michelle in either direction. But in the end, she slurred the cliched phrase, 'better to have loved and lost,' and then promptly fell asleep on her sun lounger. She woke hours later when the early morning chill took hold, only to crawl next door to her bed. Michelle had pulled a deflated lilo on top of her and was snoring.

Perhaps she will get some fresh bread on the way home and some Greek yoghurt. They can lunch together and if Michelle has not finished her letter, maybe she can help.

# Toula

The next morning, Toula does not trust the lift so she drags her case down the stairs. It thumps on each step, leaving scratch marks on the two-hundred-year-old polished planks. Leaving the awkward mass just inside the main door, she returns upstairs for her handbag.

'Yianni will be here soon,' she says. Apostolis is standing by one of the long case clocks, looking at his watch.

'I thought you asked him to be here at ten.'

'I did.' Toula looks at the clock, which says five to. Another one says it is one minute to, and yet another says it is eight minutes to the hour. Apostolis grunts and re-pockets his watch. Toula looks around the room again, double checking the cat is not still in the house. She has heard too many stories of cats locked in storage places, the poor things dying of the heat or lack of water. Well, if it rains again like it did last night, there is no need to worry about that, as there will be more puddles in the utility room and in the lift shaft. But the rain at this time of year is spasmodic and two weeks is a long time. With one last look round and satisfied that the cat is not there, she hurries to leave.

'Oh do come on, Apostolis. I would rather be standing in the street for a moment than miss the train.' Toula scoops up her handbag.

'I thought you said the train was at ten past.' Apostolis zips up his overnight bag, which is lying on the desk with a sheaf of papers on top of his clothes. He is not taking much: a change of shirt, clean socks, his toothbrush. 'It will only take the taxi two minutes to drive from here to the train station,' he adds.

Toula can feel her jaw tense and her head shakes slightly, wobbles from side to side. Why does he always need to be so argumentative, pedantic? Everything has to work to his command, his timing. She checks the kitchen one last time. The kettle is unplugged, the shutters are closed, there is no cat.

'I am going to wait downstairs. I suggest you don't use the lift. The electricians came yesterday evening when you were out buying Katerina a present and they said there is a definite fault, maybe from the rain leaking into the shaft. As if I haven't been telling them that for months.'

'It works fine for me.' Apostolis lifts a large brass key from a drawer in the desk and starts to wind the clock on the mantelpiece.

'You're not winding clocks now, are you? We need to go,' Toula shouts up the stairs behind her. She is halfway down now. 'I can hear the taxi beeping.' She continues her descent. 'Come on. And double-check your study.' She didn't check there for the cat, but then, why would the cat go there? He avoids Apostolis and anything that smells of him as if he is a disease.

The sound of Apostolis winding the clocks continues. Once on the ground floor, she pulls at her big bag, which causes the shoulder strap of her handbag to slip down her arm. Letting go of the suitcase, she saves her handbag from spilling onto the floor and Yianni comes to the rescue. He lifts her suitcase as if it is full of feathers, waits for her to exit, and slams the door closed behind him.

'Oh, Apostolis is coming,' she calls back to Yianni, but the door is already shut. No matter; the latch is easy to lift from the inside. Besides, it will stop the cat slipping in when they are not looking. Toula struggles a bit to get into the taxi. Her best skirt seems to have shrunk by hanging in the wardrobe all these years. Yianni puts her bag in the boot and looks at his watch.

'Do you want me to go and call him?' he asks.

'No, it will only annoy him.' Toula tries to wait patiently.

Yianni climbs in, tunes in the radio.

It makes her feel so tense, this last minute dashing. Apostolis never considers the people around him. Yianni might have another fare he must go and collect, the train might be early, something might impede their journey. Why does he not come?

Slipping and struggling off the backseat, she waddles back down the lane. She fiddles with her keys, picking out the right one.

# Juliet

Juliet has come into Saros early just to take her own shoes to the cobblers.

Moving from the poolside to her bed in the small hours of the morning, having put the sun umbrella up over the still-sleeping Michelle when the warm rain started to fall, chased away all chances of sleep. She spent some time tossing and turning and replaying the events of the day before over and over in her mind until eventually she accepted that sleep was unlikely and she got up. Coffee brought no clarity and her fuzzy head refused to do any work, so a trip into Saros now the rain had stopped seemed like the most productive option.

After leaving her shoes, it is still early and she desperately wants to shake off her fuddled thinking, so partly for this reason and partly out of what has now become habit, she stops at the little café for another coffee. The waiter, all smiles but casual, brings her drink out without her having to make an order.

As he sets the cup and saucer down with a *kalimera*, Juliet replies automatically but she is watching a car pull up at the end of the lane and, even from this distance, she recognises Yianni the taxi driver as he climbs out. Toula must have called him. The villagers like to give work to one another, even if the villagers no longer live in the village.

Yianni, standing by the driver's side leans through the window and beeps his horn three times. It is a while before the dark red door opens. Yianni, ever vigilant, strides across to help the old woman with her bags, guiding her to the back seat of the car.

The taxi does not set off at once. The cat, which seems to live permanently on one of the air conditioning units attached to a taverna, is there again. Perhaps it is warm there by night and cool by day. Maybe the waiter or the cook feeds the cat. One floor up on the opposite side of the lane, a woman comes out onto her balcony, jug in hand, to water her plants, the orange jug in sharp contrast to the green leaves. After the woman returns inside, water begins to drip from the bottoms of the pots and down onto the lane.

Juliet must have missed Toula getting out of the taxi again, as she is by her front door now, hand raised ready to put a key in the lock. But then she freezes, her chin angles up, poised like a bird listening.

Transfixed, Juliet cannot take her eyes away. There is no reason for her intense interest; the scene is mundane. Toula remains motionless for a good minute, then pockets her keys and turns around and shuffles back to the waiting taxi. Juliet shivers, as she has twice before at the sight of Toula in the lane, and then Toula climbs into the taxi and slams the door behind her.

# Toula

'He says he will catch the later train,' Toula tells Yianni. 'We must go or we will miss the train.' Yianni turns the radio up a fraction, starts the engine, and smoothly drives off towards the station.

## Two weeks later

## Toula

It is strange to see Saros again. It looks so small, so provincial. Toula climbs down from the train with only her handbag. She left her suitcases, her clothes in London. She will need them there next time. It will be easier to travel light.

There are taxis waiting by the open platform, but Toula has her new London shoes on, the sun is shining, as it always does in Greece, and she decides she will walk.

The sea is sparkling as it always does, but there is now a nip in the air. It is positively warm after two weeks in London.

She inhales and takes a good long look, as if she is seeing it for the first time.

It is a pretty town, there is no denying that. The palm trees, equally spaced along the harbour in front of the cafés, add vibrancy to the historic buildings. On the road that cuts between harbour and cafés, walking at a steady pace, there is a horse pulling a carriage. It is for the tourists and it adds charm to the town. It will be lovely to bring Katerina here for holidays when she is a little bigger. She would love to have a carriage ride.

The horse passes and Toula crosses the road. The cafés are all alive with Athenians down for the weekend, mostly young men with their new girlfriends. She can tell. The men are being attentive, demonstrative. They are playing to the women, who are acting as if they are used to being treated like queens, each enjoying their roles. It will be the man who forgets his part first. The girl's confidence will suffer and then she will try to gain his attention back. He will make less effort, and the downward spiral has begun.

As she nears her own building, her head begins to wobble, side to side and up and down. Toula tuts her disdain. Apart from the first day waiting at the airport to see her daughter's smiling face, her head has not wobbled, not once, nor have her hands shaken. In fact, she has felt years younger in every possible way. She even enjoyed a little flirtation with a lovely man who was apparently her daughter's boss. He had such a way with words, but then, he was of Cretan descent, and they are all so masculine down there.

The side balcony with the fig tree is still there. The crack has grown no worse. If there is a frost this winter and water gets in that crack and it freezes, the whole lot will come down. It will split right open.

Round the corner into the back lane. There is her door. She stands still and blinks. Now she is here, she is not sure she can face her home. Not alone.

After a frozen minute or two, she moves on slowly, walks straight past her door and continues to the electrician's office.

'Ah Kyria Toula, what a nice surprise.' The man behind the desk is insincere. He might well be embarrassed—how long has she been waiting for them to fix the lift?

'You will come right now,' Toula demands.

'Well, Kyria.' He shuffles some papers on his desk, procrastinating his reply.

'Now or never.' Toula feels like one of the London ladies who expect what they ask for. 'I can take the work elsewhere, and if I do, when I rewire the house, it will not be you who gets the job.' There! A bold-faced lie. She has no intention of rewiring the house.

But her words have the desired effect. The electrician is coming around his big desk, keys in hand, ready to lock up and go with her.

Even though she has this small piece of success, Toula does not speed her walk back to her house. Instead, she shuffles her feet and stops to pluck a sprig of bougainvillea. The cat is not on the air conditioning unit, or anywhere else that she can see. She hears the electrician clearing his throat impatiently, but she is in no hurry. Quite the opposite.

Once at her door, there is no more putting off the job. Keys in hand, she opens the heavy door with a shove. Little splinters of paint flick off where her shoulder has applied pressure to the moulding around the door, but she does not care. It will not be her problem soon. All she can focus on is the smell, the intense horrible smell, like rotting potatoes, but many times worse.

# Juliet

Juliet and Michelle sit at the vacant table. Two Greek women, whose faces Juliet recognises, are taking up their usual seats. They are not from the village. If they were, she would know them by name. They are from the town, which is not so big. She sees the same people over and over again, at the *laiki*—the farmer's market, in the post office, in the bank. She will have seen them somewhere. They exchange good mornings.

The days are getting cooler now, the sun has lost its intensity, and it is pleasant to sit without shade. Three weeks at this time of year is all it takes to change to a new season. It rained again last night, hissing as the soil soaked up the moisture, drumming on the roof. There were only a few drips through the old skylight window in her kitchen, which leaks when it rains hard. She must get that fixed before the winter really sets in.

Michelle checks her watch again, pulls her cardigan up her arm.

'You will be a mess if you keep looking at your watch. The train comes at ten and not before!' Juliet tells her. Michelle takes a mirror from her bag and studies her face. Shaking her head, Juliet lets out a little snort. But she does not kid herself that she is not just a little jealous. She likes having her own home, no one to answer to, and she loves her financial independence. But she is also now aware of how much she has been looking forward to Michelle being next door all winter, of being able to share the long evenings with someone, games of scrabble maybe, share a bottle of wine or a hot chocolate when it gets really cold, building up the wood fire and snuggling in—but with company. It took the edge off the thoughts of long winter nights and short winter days.

Now, it will not be that way at all. Michelle is waiting to see if her winters, all her winters, will be different, and Juliet has no doubt that they will be.

Idly, Juliet leans over and picks up a local newspaper that someone has left on the windowsill. On the front page, there are pictures of the harbour, where it extends at right angles out into the sea, to give more area for yachts to dock. It seems that this old jetty, with its modern tarmac top, complete with white lines to indicate car parking spaces, has started to subside. The water is reclaiming its own and the newspaper gives notice that it is no longer advisable or permissible to park there.

Juliet turns the page. Toula has not been in touch since she sent a postcard of Big Ben. She must have been back a week now. But then, travel can be very unsettling. She will be finding her feet, getting into a rhythm of life again, winching up things in her basket and replenishing her larder and fridge with dishes for Apostolis.

'Oh look,' Michelle says with animation.

At the end of the lane, two men with ladders are hoisting a big sign up onto the side of Toula's building.

'What on earth?' Juliet strains to see what is painted on the board. Lettering of some kind.

The waiter comes out, smiles widely at them, turns to go indoors, presumably to get their usual, but then seems to change his mind.

'Coffee? Or maybe you would like hot chocolate?'

Juliet cannot see past him to read the sign, so she turns her attention to what he has suggested.

'Yes, hot chocolate sounds good.' It isn't really cold enough, and here in the sun, she is happy to sit in her thin jumper, but the idea of a mug of steaming chocolate sounds great.

'Me too,' Michelle agrees. 'But with a dash of something stronger in mine.'

'Peppermint schnapps, rum, or whiskey?' The waiter shows no surprise at this request so early in the day. His hands rest in the front pocket of his wrap-around white apron. He has the easy manner of a man content with himself.

'Oh, peppermint schnapps sound delicious.' Michelle nods enthusiastically and then checks her watch again as he wanders off inside. The men are struggling with the sign. 'Have you heard anything from Toula since she came back?' she asks, but without much interest.

'No, well, yes. I got a postcard from her saying she was in London, that she was having great time and that she would be very happy to never come home. But that was two weeks ago. I am just a little surprised that she has not been in touch since she got home.'

'That's how it is with great holidays, eh Juliet? You never want to go home. Maybe she didn't. Maybe she stayed.' Michelle is teasing. As Juliet smiles, only one side of her mouth twists, her gaze remaining on the men and their ladders. Health and safety would have a field day. The two ladders have nothing to stop them from sliding on the cobbles. One ladder is not vertical, its sideways pitch halted by a stone that juts out of the otherwise smooth wall. The men are trying to climb the ladder whilst each heaving one end of the sign up, but really, it is too big and too awkward to be handled like that. It would be better to be passed up once the men have climbed their ladders, or even winched up somehow.

The waiter returns. He puts down two tall glass mugs of thick chocolate topped with white froth and sprigs of fresh mint. But both Juliet and Michelle are concentrating on the dangerous manoeuvre, pulling faces at every possible horror that could be about to happen, but, somehow, never quite does.

'Ah,' the waiter says as if he has been expecting such a scene. 'It has come.'

Michelle speaks first. 'What is it?'

'My cousin-in-law, he has an *epigraphes* business,' the waiter says proudly.

'A sign-writing shop,' Juliet translates for Michelle, whose Greek is nowhere near as fluent as her own.

'Oh, but what does it say?'

The waiter makes a sound as if he is incredulous that they do not know before saying, 'It is for sale!'

'The house?' It is Juliet who now sounds incredulous.

'Yes.' The waiter folds his arms across his chest and watches Laurel and Hardy trying to kill themselves with the plywood sign, which is getting lifted out of their grasp by the slight breeze. 'The house, the shop beneath. The van came last week and took the furniture to an antiques place in Athens. Everything.'

Juliet stares intently at the sign as if this will fill in all the blanks in her knowledge.

'But Toula, her husband, where are they going?'

The waiter turns to look at her and whistles through his teeth.

'You didn't hear?' He is shaking his head, and there is a sad look in his eyes as he goes inside, leaving Juliet and Michelle none the wiser. She could ask the men putting up the sign, but would they know? The only phone number she has for Toula is the house phone, so if she isn't there…

'Here.' The waiter has returned and offers a well-thumbed local paper folded over with a picture of Toula's house at the top and an inset picture of an old man. The caption underneath says it is Kyrios Apostolis Maraveyas, Toula's husband.

'Read it out loud,' Michelle demands, wiping her froth moustache off her upper lip and declaring the chocolate good.

'Oh my God!' Juliet exclaims.

'Come on, what?' Michelle pulls at the paper to see the picture.

'That is unbelievable.'

'What, what is?'

'Listen. Toula Maraveyas returned home from visiting her family in London last week to find the lift in her house stuck between floors. On calling the electrician, the lift was lowered to the ground floor and when the doors were opened…'

# Toula

The smell is all invasive. She felt her stomach turn over. The electrician has one arm over his nose and mouth, working hard with his free hand.

'That's a dead animal, that is,' he tells her, struggling to get the lift open. 'I'll get that out for you and then when it has aired a bit, I can work on the electrics.' And with these words, the doors swing outwards.

The electrician's jaw drops open and his hand covers his nose and mouth. The flies come at them like angry hornets. His screwdriver clangs as it hits the lift's metal floor. Half a step closer, one step away. Turning, he dry retches, eyes closed.

'Don't look.' He makes a gasp for breath. He steps between Toula and the lift, hands on her shoulders, turning her, pushing her. But it is too late, she has seen. Her fingers drop from her own nose.

An eye socket. One gaping, dark, empty eye socket. A dried, black stain beneath the backside. The legs twisted to fit the space. The head at a strange angle, tilted, against the wall. Skin drawn over bone. Epidermis slippage on the jawline. Indented cheeks. A cockroach wriggles, squeezes out between the swollen black tongue and the dark purple lips, scuttles over parched chin, down inside his shirt. The cat freezes in motion over the exposed ankle, chewing the remaining mouthful.

Toula squeals and her body turns but her head remains still. Her eyes will not stop staring. It isn't real. But it is. His suit, stained, gradating darker near the floor. It is getting dirty, lying in the pool of... The smell is so intense. Her hand returns to her nose. The electrician rushes outside, throws up. The cat, narrowing its eyes against the light, smelling the fresh air, rushes for freedom.

But still, Toula cannot look away. The remaining eye open, veiled opaque. Unreal. Glass, unfocused, lifeless. Fixed on his bone-protruding hand that rests on his chest. Fingers grasped, firmly clenched, on his open watch.

All that can be heard is the steady ticking of his repeater, but for Apostolis, there is no time left at all.

# Juliet

Juliet gasps then reads aloud, 'They found the body of Kyrios Apostolis Maraveyas.' She pauses to let this information sink in. 'The post mortem shows that he died of,' another pause as she translates the word into English in her head before speaking, 'dehydration, having been imprisoned, it appeared, in the lift for the entire two weeks his wife was away.'

'Oh how horrible!' Michelle comments.

Juliet shivers. It starts in her shoulders and descends the length of her spine before the hairs on the back of her neck stand up. She had watched as Toula drove away in the taxi that day. How long after that was it before Apostolis was stuck in the lift? But didn't Toula say they would take the same train up to Athens? She did! Juliet shivers again.

And what was that with Toula listening at her door before leaving? Not talking, not answering, just listening.

'Does it say anything else?' Michelle asks. The men have attached one corner of the sign to the wall and now concentrate on getting it level.

'No.' Juliet looks at the date of the newspaper and then picks up a newer copy from the next table. It is the subsequent release. She turns the first and second page and folds the newspaper back on itself.

'This is this week's newspaper.'

'Kyrios Apostolis Maraveyas left his estate to his wife and his nephew, Emilianos Maraveyas, who is also a joint benefactor of his considerable life insurance.' She turns the page for more, but there isn't any.

'You reading about Kyria Maraveyas?' one of the ladies at the next table asks.

Juliet nods sadly.

'A terrible tragedy.' She nods her head sadly in response. 'She is selling the lot, you know.' Now it is her friend who nods, but in a matter of fact way, as if such a choice was the only logical next step. 'The house and all her belongings. She is moving to London.'

Juliet opens her mouth to say something, but no sound comes out.

'She has arranged to buy a small mews in South Kensington, to be near her daughter,' the talkative woman's friend chimes in. 'But what is a 'mews,' I wonder.' A little knot of muscle forms between her eyes. The ladies pay and leave, wishing Juliet a good day. 'Did you understand all that?' Juliet asks Michelle, who seems content with however much she did grasp.

'I think it is a case of be careful of what you wish for. Didn't you say she was not totally happy and wanted to see more of her daughter?' Michelle replies.

Juliet cannot shake the image of Toula listening through the door before getting into the taxi.

'Oh my God, I've got to go!' Michelle leaps up, catching the table with her knee, causing the hot chocolates to spill into their saucers.

'Wish me luck,' she shouts back at Juliet as she trots towards the station.

'Luck,' Juliet calls. In a few minutes, Michelle will be in Dino's arms. Their chests pressed against each other, their hearts synchronising and beating as one. They each will declare their undying love, and another partnership will be born.

How many years will it take for Michelle, or worse, Dino, to be listening at the door as the other cries for their freedom?

Juliet may have times when she is lonely, she may have times when it all feels a little pointless without someone to share all she does, but one thing she is absolutely certain of: she is not ready to risk having to pay such a high price. She is not that desperate. Not yet, anyway.

She mops at the hot chocolate with a paper napkin.

'You want me to help?' the waiter asks.

'No, thank you. I am fine.'

'Can I get you anything else?' he persists.

'No, really, I am okay.'

'Yes, fine,' the waiter says in broken English

Juliet is surprised to hear him speak to her in English and she looks up at him. He pulls out Michelle's chair and sits down. Juliet moves her knees slightly away from him.

'This the Juliet fine. I have been told.' With the flicker of a smile playing around his mouth, Juliet is not sure what to make of the exchange. 'And I believe her.' His accent is thick, his English not so good.

Juliet blinks as she tries to work out if she is meant to know who he is talking about.

'So, now she is gone, I can take her lesson period, yes? And money, it is not a problem.' He holds out his hand to Juliet. 'Emilianos,' he smiles, introducing himself.

She is not sure if it is the words he has spoken or the way he smiles as he looks in her eyes. She tries not to have this response, but it is almost as if she has no choice. Juliet shivers.

Made in the USA
San Bernardino, CA
04 January 2017